Good Night, Sleep Tight, Don't Let the Bedbugs Bite!

Good Night, Sleep Tight, Don't Let the Bedbugs Bite!

Diane deGroat

HI-DEE-HO

CAMPGROUND

SeaStar Books · New York

SEASTAR BOOKS
A division of NORTH-SOUTH BOOKS INC.

First published in the United States by SeaStar Books, a division of North-South Books Inc., New York.
Published simultaneously in Canada, Australia, and New Zealand by North-South Books,
an imprint of Nord-Süd Verlag AG, Gossau Zürich, Switzerland.

Library of Congress Cataloging-in-Publication Data is available.
The artwork for this book was prepared by using watercolors.
The text for this book is set in 14-point Korinna.

ISBN 1-58717-128-7 (trade edition)
1 3 5 7 9 HC 10 8 6 4 2
ISBN 1-58717-129-5 (library edition)
1 3 5 7 9 LE 10 8 6 4 2

Printed in Singapore

For more information about our books, and the authors and artists who create them,
visit our web site: www.northsouth.com

To Norm . . . a happy camper

G ilbert was excited. Everyone from his day camp was going on an overnight trip to Camp Hi-Dee-Ho.

Mother helped him pack his favorite pajamas, bug spray, and a flashlight. "Don't forget Teddy," she said, holding up Gilbert's stuffed possum.

"I'm not taking Teddy," Gilbert said. "Sleep-away camp is for big kids."

Frank was worried when Gilbert met him on the bus.
He said, "My brother told me there's a ghost at Camp
Hi-Dee-Ho!"

Patty peered over her seat and said, "He's just trying to
scare you."

But Lewis said, "It's true. Everybody knows about the Hi-Dee-Ho ghost. You'd better watch out, Gilbert. He might jump out and yell *BOO!*"

But Gilbert said, "You can't scare me, Lewis. There's no such thing as ghosts."

After a long ride, the bus pulled into the Hi-Dee-Ho campground. Gilbert and Frank unpacked in the boys' cabin. "Bunk beds!" Frank said, taking a top bunk. "I like sleep-away camp!"

"Me, too," said Gilbert, taking the bottom bunk.

But Lewis said, "Just wait until dark. Then we'll see how much you like it."

"You'd better not try to scare us," Gilbert said, "or you'll be sorry!"

"*Boo hoo*," said Lewis. "I'm scared."

For the rest of the afternoon they swam and canoed and hiked with the big kids. Gilbert was hot and thirsty after all the activity. He drank three cups of juice at suppertime.

"Ooooh, you're drinking bug juice!" Lewis said as he passed Gilbert's table.

Gilbert looked at his empty cup. He was sure
it was fruit juice, but he drank a big glass of water
to wash it down, just in case.

After supper they roasted marshmallows over the campfire. Lewis said, "Let's tell ghost stories!" He was shining his flashlight under his chin, making scary faces.

Frank whispered in Gilbert's ear, "I don't think I want to hear a ghost story."

"Me either," said Gilbert quietly.

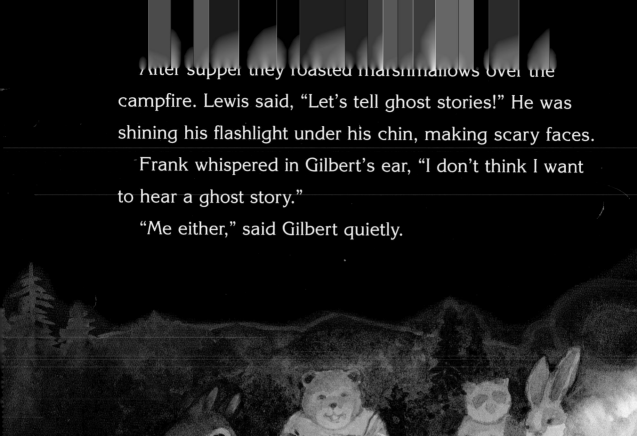

But one of the big kids had already stood up. He said, "The campers who have been here all summer have heard this story, but I'll share it with our guests." He started speaking in a spooky voice, "What I'm about to tell you is all true. It happened many years ago, right here at Camp Hi-Dee-Ho."

"It was a dark and stormy night. A camper went out to get some water from the bathroom. He had his canteen and a candle, but the wind blew the candle out—*POOF!*—and he lost his way. He wandered for days, weeks, and finally . . . years. They say he's still lurking around here as . . . A GHOST!"

Everyone jumped. Patty's eyes were very wide. Gilbert's were wider.

"They call him Lost Leonard, and sometimes you can hear him in the woods at night, banging his canteen. Like THIS!" The storyteller banged a metal can against a rock— *CLANKITY CLANK CLANK!*

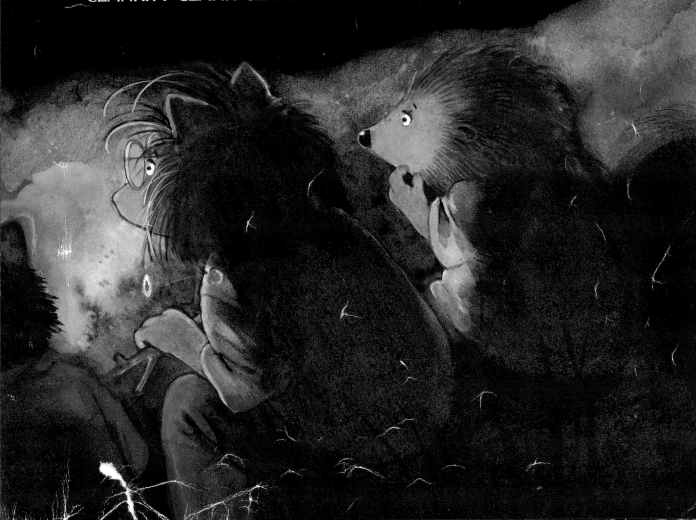

Then he crouched down and said softly, "And sometimes, if you listen very carefully, you can hear Lost Leonard crying—*Booo hooooo. Boooo hoooooo.*"

No one made a sound. Gilbert held his breath. Then right behind him came a loud . . .

"BOO!"

Gilbert flew off his seat. He turned and saw Lewis laughing at him. "Lewis!" he said. "That's not funny!"

"What a scaredy-cat," Lewis said.

"I am not," Gilbert answered. But his heart was beating very quickly.

"Lights out," the counselor said when the campers were finally in their bunks. "Good night. . . . Sleep tight!"

"Don't let the bedbugs bite!" Lewis answered.

Everybody shut off their flashlights. Except Gilbert. What if there *were* bedbugs in his bunk? He checked inside his sleeping bag. There weren't any bugs in it, but there was something soft and furry there—Teddy! His mother must have slipped it in when Gilbert wasn't looking.

"Hey, scaredy-cat!" Lewis shouted from the other side of the room. "Lights out!"

Gilbert turned off his flashlight. He closed his eyes. He opened his eyes. He closed them again. It was so dark, he couldn't tell if his eyes were open or closed!

He hugged his Teddy tightly until he finally fell asleep.

But in the middle of the night Gilbert was wide awake again. He wished he hadn't had so much juice. Now he had to go to the bathroom. He was afraid to go out in the dark, but he was more afraid of wetting the bed. Lewis would make fun of him again!

The more he thought about it, the more he had to go. "Frank?" he whispered. Frank snored. He was sound asleep. Gilbert would have to go alone.

Carefully, he followed the path to the bathroom, but it seemed much longer than he remembered. He could easily get lost. Maybe he would end up wandering around the woods for years, just like Lost Leonard!

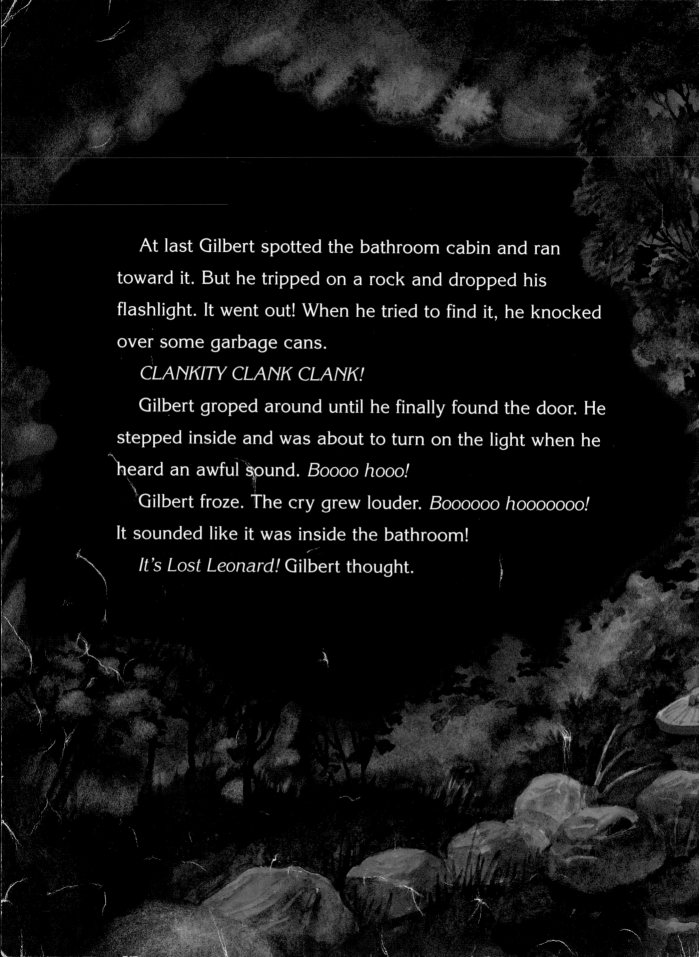

At last Gilbert spotted the bathroom cabin and ran toward it. But he tripped on a rock and dropped his flashlight. It went out! When he tried to find it, he knocked over some garbage cans.

CLANKITY CLANK CLANK!

Gilbert groped around until he finally found the door. He stepped inside and was about to turn on the light when he heard an awful sound. *Boooo hooo!*

Gilbert froze. The cry grew louder. *Boooooo hooooooo!* It sounded like it was inside the bathroom!

It's Lost Leonard! Gilbert thought.

Gilbert tried to run, but his feet wouldn't budge.
Instead, he held his breath and flipped the light switch.

"*Yeeoow!*" Gilbert screamed.

"*Yeeoow!*" someone else screamed at the same time.
But it wasn't a ghost. It was Lewis! His hair was sticking
straight up and he clutched a stuffed animal.

Lewis sniffed. "Gilbert! You'd better hide—Lost Leonard is out there! Didn't you hear that clanking noise?"

Gilbert could see that Lewis was very frightened. He felt sorry for him, but not sorry enough to tell him the truth.

Gilbert bravely opened the door and called, "Hello? Leonard? Are you out there?" There was no answer. "I think he's gone," Gilbert said. "I don't hear any clanking."

"You're right," said Lewis, peeking out the door. But he waited for Gilbert to go out first, just in case.

As they walked back to the cabin, Lewis said, "I wasn't really crying, you know. I think I had something in my eye."

Gilbert said, "That happens to me sometimes, too." Then he stopped to pick up his flashlight and his Teddy. He held up the stuffed possum and said, "My mother packed this in my bag."

Lewis nodded and said, "Mine, too."

On the bus ride home, Patty said, "Sleep-away camp was fun." Then she added, "Except for the ghost story. I kept thinking I heard noises in the middle of the night."

Frank said, "I'd be scared if I heard Lost Leonard!"

Lewis laughed and said, "What a bunch of scaredy-cats."
But when Gilbert turned around and yelled "*BOO!*" Lewis
jumped out of his seat.

And he was quiet for the rest of the ride home.

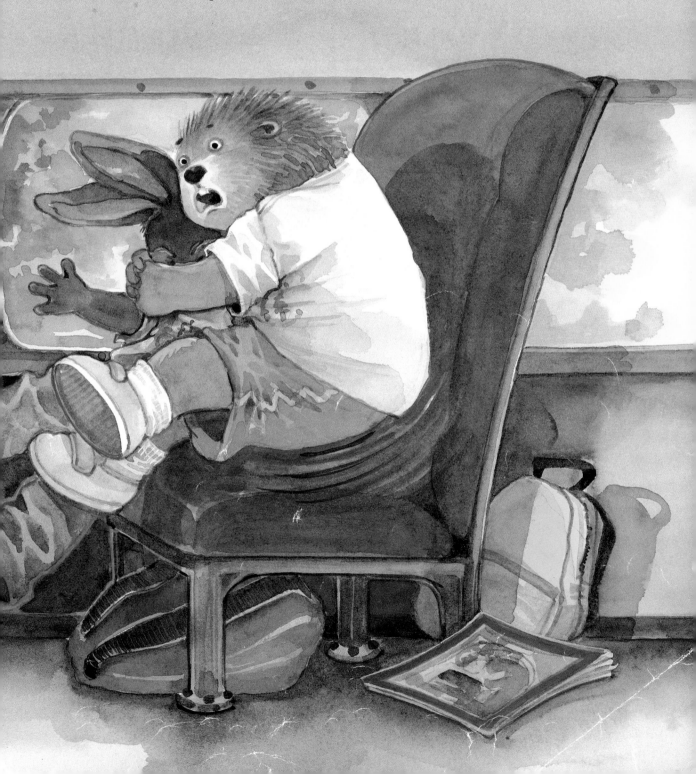